A Note to Parents and Caregivers:

Read-it! Readers are for children who are just starting on the amazing road to reading. These beautiful books support both the acquisition of reading skills and the love of books. In some books, there are common sounds at the beginning, the ending, or even in the middle of many familiar words. It is good preparation for reading to help students listen for and repeat these sounds as part of having fun with words.

The RED LEVEL presents familiar topics using common words and repeating sentence patterns.

The BLUE LEVEL presents new ideas using a larger vocabulary and varied sentence structure.

The YELLOW LEVEL presents more challenging ideas, a broad vocabulary, and wide variety in sentence structure.

The GREEN LEVEL presents more complex ideas, an extended vocabulary range, and expanded language structures.

When sharing a book with your child, read in short stretches, pausing often to talk about the pictures. Have your child turn the pages and point to the pictures and familiar words. And be sure to reread favorite stories or parts of stories.

There is no right or wrong way to share books with children. Find time to read with your child, and pass on the legacy of literacy.

Adria F. Klein, Ph.D.
Professor Emeritus
California State University
San Bernardino, California

Managing Editors: Bob Temple, Catherine Neitge
Creative Director: Terri Foley
Editors: Jerry Ruff, Patricia Stockland
Editorial Adviser: Mary Lindeen
Designer: Amy Bailey Muehlenhardt
Storyboard development: Charlene DeLage
Page production: Picture Window Books
The illustrations in this book were prepared digitally.

Picture Window Books
5115 Excelsior Boulevard
Suite 232
Minneapolis, MN 55416
877-845-8392
www.picturewindowbooks.com

Printed in the United States of America.

Library of Congress Cataloging-in-Publication Data
Blackaby, Susan.
Classroom cookout / by Susan Blackaby ; illustrated by Amy Bailey
Muehlenhardt.
p. cm. — (Read-it! readers classroom tales)
Summary: Mrs. Shay asks her students to tally how many hot dogs they
will need for the class picnic.
ISBN 1-4048-0583-4 (hardcover)
[1. Picnicking—Fiction. 2. Frankfurters—Fiction. 3. Schools—Fiction.]
I. Muehlenhardt, Amy Bailey, 1974- ill. II. Title. III. Series.
PZ7.B5318Cl 2004
[E]—dc22
2004007389

Classroom Cookout

By Susan Blackaby

Illustrated by Amy Bailey Muehlenhardt

Special thanks to our advisers for their expertise:

Adria F. Klein, Ph.D.
Professor Emeritus, California State University
San Bernardino, California

Susan Kesselring, M.A.
Literacy Educator
Rosemount-Apple Valley-Eagan (Minnesota) School District

PiCTURE WiNDOW BOOKS
Minneapolis, Minnesota

"We need to plan for our class cookout," said Mrs. Shay.

"Let's play tag," said Kat.

"Let's play basketball," said Jess.

Class Cookout

"Let's play kickball," said Vic.

"Let's eat hot dogs," said Bob.

"This will be so fun," said Sunny.

"How many hot dogs can you kids eat?" asked Mrs. Shay. "We need to find out how many packs to get."

"There are 10 in a pack," said Kat.

"We will need lots," said Bob.

Mrs. Shay gave Bob a job.
"Make one tally mark for each hot
dog," said Mrs. Shay.

Mrs. Shay made five tally marks to show Bob how.

"Got it," said Bob.

Bob thought, I can eat lots of hot dogs. I can gobble at least a pack. He made five more tally marks.

10

Bob thought, I will put one more tally mark for me, just in case. Bob put another tally mark on the page.

"How many hot dogs can you eat?"
asked Bob.

"I can eat six," said Vic.

"I can eat three," said Kat.

Bob made nine more tally marks.

"Have we got ketchup?" asked Jess.
"Yes," said Bob.

"Then I can eat gobs of dogs," said Jess.

"I do not like hot dogs," said Sunny. "I just like buns with mustard. I can eat a bunch of buns."

"OK," said Bob. "I will not make a mark for Sunny. I will make seven marks for Jess."

"That will be plenty," said Jess.

Bob asked the other kids in the class. He had lots of tally marks on the page. He showed the page to Mrs. Shay.

"Let's add these up," said Mrs. Shay.

The kids helped Mrs. Shay count.
They drew a ring around each set
of 10.

Each ring stood for one pack of hot dogs.

"I do not think you kids can eat this many hot dogs," said Mrs. Shay. "Let's count again."

"There are 20 kids in this class," said Mrs. Shay. "Each kid gets one hot dog. We need two packs."

"What if each kid got two hot dogs?" Bob asked.

"Then we need four packs,"
said Kat.

Bob thought, I can eat lots more hot dogs than that. "Maybe we need more packs," he said.

"I just want the bun with mustard," said Sunny. "Bob can have my hot dogs."

"Lots of hot dogs might make me sick," said Vic. "Bob can have one of my hot dogs, too."

"Four packs will be plenty," said Jess. "Bob gets all the extra hot dogs he wants."

"OK!" said Mrs. Shay.

"Hot dog!" said Bob.

Levels for *Read-it!* Readers

Read-it! Readers help children practice early reading skills with brightly illustrated stories.

 Red Level: Familiar topics with frequently used words and repeating patterns.

I Am in Charge of Me by Dana Meachen Rau
Let's Share by Dana Meachen Rau

 Blue Level: New ideas with a larger vocabulary and a variety of language structures.

At the Beach by Patricia M. Stockland
The Playground Snake by Brian Moses
The Word of the Day by Susan Blackaby

 Yellow Level: Challenging ideas with an expanded vocabulary and a wide variety of sentences.

A Fire Drill with Mr. Dill by Susan Blackaby
Hatching Chicks by Susan Blackaby
Marvin, The Blue Pig by Karen Wallace
Moo! by Penny Dolan
Pippin's Big Jump by Hilary Robinson
A Pup Shows Up by Susan Blackaby
The Queen's Dragon by Anne Cassidy
Tired of Waiting by Dana Meachen Rau

 Green Level: More complex ideas with an extended vocabulary range and expanded language structures.

Classroom Cookout by Susan Blackaby
Clever Cat by Karen Wallace
Flora McQuack by Penny Dolan
Izzie's Idea by Jillian Powell
Naughty Nancy by Anne Cassidy
The Roly-Poly Rice Ball by Penny Dolan
Sausages! by Anne Adeney
Sunny Bumps the Drum by Susan Blackaby
The Truth About Hansel and Gretel by Karina Law

A complete list of *Read-it!* Readers is available on our Web site:
www.picturewindowbooks.com